Yaw Ababio Boateng

Kodua's Ark

Illustrated by
Barry Wilkinson

CHELSEA HOUSE PUBLISHERS
New York • Philadelphia

Series Editor: Rod Nesbitt

This edition published 1995 by
Chelsea House Publishers, a division of Main Line Book Co.,
300 Park Avenue South, New York, N.Y. 10010
by arrangement with Heinemann

First published by Heinemann International Literature and Textbooks in 1994

ISBN 0-7910-3161-6

Printed and bound in Great Britain by
Cox & Wyman Ltd, Reading, Berkshire

1 3 5 7 9 10 8 6 4 2

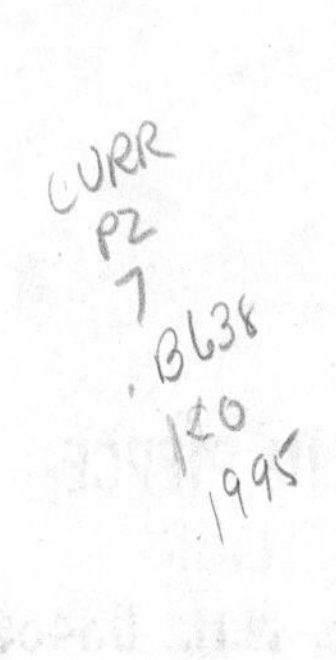

CHAPTER ONE

Everyone in the village of Mantu knew Kojo Kodua. From the youngest school child to the oldest man and woman, everyone simply called him KK. Indeed the children of Mantu loved to follow Kodua about shouting, 'KK boozeman! KK drinkerman!'

In the daytime he was always at Mame Ataa's palm wine bar drinking palm wine or playing draughts. People laughed. If Kodua could not be found at Mame Ataa's bar in the daytime, then he was probably dead, they said.

Nobody knew exactly how old Kodua was. Not that it mattered much to anyone. The children thought he was grown up, while the adults thought he was childish. Kodua himself did not know how old he was. His parents once told him, before they deserted him, that he was born at the time of the last great famine in Mantu. But everybody agreed that there had not been a famine in Mantu for nearly fifty years! If people asked, Kodua told them he was eighteen.

Kodua woke up at dawn as usual. He looked around and went back to sleep. There was no reason to get up early anyway when there was nothing to do.

By the time he finally woke up, the sun was up and shining. His best and only friend, Kwasi Nyamesem, was still asleep on the mat beside him. People often said that they looked alike. Some even said that they could be twins. But Kodua was much taller than his friend. He sat on the mat and looked at his sleeping friend. Then he wondered if he really looked like that. He saw a hard, rugged face with narrow cheeks, a large abdomen sitting on long, thin legs. He felt his own face and protruding belly and shook his head.

Kodua shook the sad thoughts away. He kicked his friend and shouted, 'Get up, you lazy devil.'

But Nyamesem replied with a grunt and rolled over. Kodua kicked him again, and pulled away the torn blanket. This time Nyamesem started to sit up.

'What's the time?' he asked sleepily.

'Ask me when you buy a watch,' Kodua retorted.

'You know what I mean,' Nyamesem yawned. 'How high is the sun?'

'High enough. Get up and let's go,' Kodua said.

Nyamesem finally stood up and asked his friend, 'Where to?'

'To Mame Ataa's bar, of course. My stomach is crying for palm wine.'

The thought of palm wine brought a smile to Kodua's face. He went out of the room ahead of

Nyamesem and fetched water from the barrel in the courtyard. He was grateful for the rainy season. For the past month neither he nor Nyamesem had had to fetch water from the river.

Nyamesem came to wash his face. He took a long piece of chewing stick from his pocket, broke it and threw one piece to Kodua.

'Palm wine will kill us oo!' he exclaimed suddenly. Then he gave a high laugh. Kodua joined in the laughter and the two laughed and laughed as if they had no troubles in the world. But they had troubles. They lived in an old house all by themselves. They had no money and no friends in the village of Mantu. Even so, they were sometimes happy.

'Palm wine go kill us oo!' Kodua laughed in pidgin English and slapped his friend's back. But even as he laughed he knew that there were other things that could kill them. Three-quarters of the house was in ruins and there were big cracks in the wall of the only room. The wall could collapse and kill them in their sleep.

He suddenly remembered a job that they had to do whenever it rained heavily, as it had done last night. Still chewing on the stick, he grabbed Nyamesem's wrist and pulled him back into the room. He pointed to the tins scattered around the mud floor. They were carefully arranged to collect rainwater from the fifteen major leaks in the roof.

'You collect from this side and I will collect from that side,' Kodua said with a smile. He always made sure that he collected from the side with six tins while Nyamesem collected the other nine tins. They took the tins in twos and emptied them into a bucket beside the full barrel. When they finished the job, they were ready to leave the house and face another day.

They couldn't have chosen a worse time to leave the house. As soon as they got into the small lane in front of the house Kodua saw several school children coming in their direction. He realised that it was probably break time for them. Kodua looked this way and that.

'Let's turn left and get away from them,' he said.

They turned left into a path that led to the river. But it was too late. Some of the children had seen them.

'KK boozeman, KK drinkerman!' some began to chant. Kodua walked faster.

'KK boozeman, KK drinkerman!!' The chants got louder as more school children joined in.

'Leave me alone, all of you!' Kodua shouted. But it was more like a plea. This only brought more laughter and more shouts. Not knowing quite what to do, Kodua started off again, this time turning towards the village centre and Mame Ataa's bar. But the children followed him. Now there were so many children that they were making a tremendous noise. Several adults came out of their houses to watch. Some even joined in.

After they had gone several metres, one of the bigger boys got brave. He went behind Kodua and pulled hard at his shirt sleeve. There was a tearing sound. Half of the long sleeve on the right side was now torn and hanging loose.

Kodua tried to grab the boy by throwing himself after him. But the boy jumped aside and Kodua came crashing down. There was more loud laughter from the children as Nyamesem tried to help Kodua up. And as if this was not enough, some of the boys began to throw stones at them.

When a stone hit Kodua on the chest, he went wild. He picked up a stone himself and threw it into the crowd of children. Someone screamed in pain and suddenly they all ran away.

'Let's go to Mame Ataa's bar for something more interesting,' Nyamesem said.

'Now you're talking,' said Kodua, thinking about palm wine.

◇

He went behind Kodua and pulled hard at his shirt sleeve.

For a Thursday morning, Mame Ataa's bar was quite full. Only two of the five benches were empty. As soon as Kodua and Nyamesem entered, everyone burst out laughing and chanting, 'KK boozeman.' This really annoyed Kodua. Men who drank more than he did were calling him a boozeman. True, he liked palm wine but he didn't drink that much because he seldom had enough money to buy as much as he really wanted. And yet everyone picked on him and called him a boozeman.

Kodua shouted a general greeting across the room and approached the counter. He looked at Mame Ataa and she frowned. She turned away to fetch palm wine for a customer. He watched her roll along, her fat arms barely swinging. It had never ceased to amaze Kodua that a human being could be so fat. It was said that she had to go sideways in order to go through doors. Kodua had wanted to see this for himself. But Mame Ataa had made all the doors in the bar very wide, and she could pass through them without any difficulty.

Mame Ataa ignored Kodua and served two other people. Finally when there were no other people to serve, she turned to Kodua.

'What do you want?' She sat down slowly.

'A bottle of palm wine, please, Mame Ataa,'

Kodua said, looking at the bottles neatly arranged on a shelf.

Mame Ataa held out her hand and said, 'Money first!'

He looked this way and that and whispered, 'I'll let you have it tomorrow.'

'Tomorrow, tomorrow. Always tomorrow!'

'Please, Mame Ataa. Just one bottle,' Kodua pleaded.

Mame Ataa got up slowly from her chair and Kodua could hear her knees creak. She walked slowly to an inner room and returned a few minutes later with a piece of paper. She placed the paper in front of him and pointed to the long, badly drawn lines. There were ten of them.

'Ten bottles, no pay! Now you say tomorrow. I should throw you out,' she said in her deep voice.

Meanwhile Nyamesem, who had gone to sit on one of the empty benches, came up to join Kodua at the counter.

'Let's go home,' he suggested.

'Home! I must have some palm wine.'

'All right, let's wait here. Maybe some kind person will buy us a drink,' said Nyamesem. He took Kodua's arm and pulled him to the bench where he himself had been sitting.

Suddenly the door of the bar burst open.

Everyone watched in silence as a well-dressed man accompanied by two women entered. The man was called Owusu Bempah. But everyone called him Manager Bempah or simply Manager. He was the richest man in Mantu and the surrounding villages, owning farms and the only two shops in Mantu. He also owned the only private car in Mantu. Naturally nobody wanted to anger him by calling him Owusu Bempah. So they gave him the important title of Manager.

Most of the drinkers stood up as a sign of respect as soon as the man entered. Some greeted him excitedly, calling to him. He waved and told everyone to sit down.

Mame Ataa came from behind the counter.

'What can I get you, Manager?' she asked.

'Six bottles, please, Mame Ataa,' Bempah said, still standing near the middle of the room, looking around. Kodua saw his chance.

'Please, Manager, come and sit here,' he said, indicating the empty bench near where they sat. Then he noticed that the reason most people had avoided that seat was because a lot of palm wine had been spilt on it. Quickly he removed his shirt and wiped the palm wine off the bench.

Bempah and the two women sat on the clean bench without even saying thank you.

'I suppose you want a reward?' he asked Kodua.

'Two bottles will do, sir, Manager,' Kodua replied quickly, putting his damp shirt back on.

'Two bottles? You must be joking. You have to earn that. Let's see.' He thought for a moment. 'All right, if you can entertain my two guests here, I'll buy you two bottles of palm wine.'

'Thank you, Manager,' Kodua said, gratefully. He looked at the two women. They were probably no older than he was and certainly young enough to be Bempah's daughters. People said that he was planning to marry a fourth wife and that the two girls were competing to be the lucky one.

Now everybody was watching with interest. For two bottles of free palm wine, Kodua would do his best.

'I'm going to tell a funny story,' he began. 'There was this farm labourer who was bitten by an earthworm. He thought it was a snake so he went to see a herbalist. The herbalist said, "Earthworms don't bite because they have no teeth!" Ha ha ha!'

There was a funny silence when he finished. Then all of a sudden, when everybody realised that the joke was not funny, they started to laugh. All except Bempah's girls. Bempah himself seemed to be laughing the loudest.

Pleased, Kodua went to demand his reward.

'I asked you to entertain these girls, not me,' Bempah said.

Kodua told another story, then another and another. Each time everyone but the girls laughed. After about ten minutes, Bempah himself came to stand in the middle of the room. There was silence, then applause.

'I'm going to tell a funny story now,' he began. 'It's about a funny man, or was he a boy? Anyway this boy had a hard face, a big belly and legs like matchsticks. He looked like a he-goat.' He turned to look at Kodua and smiled. 'In fact this boy was called KK ...'

At that everyone burst into the usual chant of 'KK boozeman, KK drinkerman'. Then everyone laughed. Even Nyamesem laughed. But the two girls still refused to laugh.

Kodua was embarrassed but, as Bempah went back to his seat, he was determined to earn the two bottles of palm wine. Suddenly he had an idea.

'I'm going to dance,' he announced and immediately started. He couldn't remember the last time he danced. And yet, so determined was he, that even without music he danced. Then he stood on his head and promptly fell down. There was more laughter. Finally even Bempah seemed to have had enough. He stood up and raised his

'I'm going to dance,' he announced and immediately started.

hands, and the laughter died down slowly.

'I think KK has earned his drinks,' he said. He took a wad of notes from his pocket and took out a five hundred cedi note. He threw it to Kodua who caught it quickly.

'Thank you, Manager. Thank you very much.'

'Well, you don't actually deserve the money since you couldn't make my guests laugh. But I am a generous man, as everyone in Mantu knows ...' Bempah stopped as if he was expecting applause. And applause he got from several of the men in the bar. Even Mame Ataa applauded. When the applause died down Bempah beckoned to the two girls and the three walked towards the door of the bar. As he passed Kodua, he slapped him lightly on the shoulder.

'You ought to do this more often,' he said. 'It's the only useful thing you can do.' With that he and the girls walked out of the bar.

Kodua stood up feeling very silly. But he was grateful to have the money. It would buy as much as five bottles of palm wine. Manager was a very generous man even if he was a bit proud. Nyamesem joined him promptly and the two walked up to the counter.

'Three bottles of palm wine, please, Mame Ataa. No, make it four!' Kodua ordered. Mame Ataa smiled and stretched out her hand.

'No problem,' Kodua said. 'Here is five hundred cedis.' He slapped the money on the counter and Mame Ataa collected it.

'Thank you,' she said. 'Now you only owe me five hundred cedis.'

Kodua was shocked. But he pretended not to understand.

'You understand all right. You owed me the money for ten bottles of palm wine. Now you've paid for five. That leaves five.'

'Don't do that to me, Mame Ataa. Please.' But Mame Ataa just shook her head.

'I'll never give you anything on credit again,' she said. 'You can never pay.'

'I'll pay you next week.'

'Where will you get the money? Who'll give it to you?'

'I'll earn it myself,' Kodua said softly.

Mame Ataa laughed and said, 'You? You'll always be poor, and one of these days people are going to get fed up helping you. Learn to stand on your own two feet.'

Kodua knew that Mame Ataa would not give him the drink. He took Nyamesem's arm and the two walked quietly out of the bar. They walked in silence until they came to the main street. Today was a market day and a few trucks could be seen loading or unloading goods. There was a lot of red mud everywhere because of the recent rains. The two walked carefully along the edge of the dirt road, avoiding puddles of water in the potholes.

'Mame Ataa is a wicked woman,' Kodua said suddenly.

'Why?' asked Nyamesem. 'She just took what belonged to her.' He laughed.

'Don't be stupid, Kwasi. That money was mine. You know I had to make an idiot of myself to earn it.'

'But we owe the woman too.'

'We're not the only people who owe her, are we? Most of the people in the bar owe her. Yet she allowed them to drink. Isaac, Korankye, TK. All of them owe her.' He stopped and thought for a while. 'What's wrong with me?'

Before Nyamesem could reply, a car hurried past them, splashing muddy water all over them. Some of the water got into Kodua's eyes. As he wiped his face, he saw Manager Bempah's car turning the corner.

'He did that on purpose,' Kodua said. But Nyamesem said nothing. He also seemed to be thinking hard.

'It's tough to be poor,' he said suddenly.

Kodua couldn't agree with him more. Suddenly he said, 'Nyamesem, we must stop being poor.'

'Stop being poor? What do you mean? How do you stop being poor?'

Nyamesem started to laugh but Kodua didn't laugh. He had a strange feeling. A voice was telling him that it is possible to stop being poor. But how? How did you stop being poor? You needed someone rich to help. But most of the well-off were busy trying to keep the poor down.

They walked along in silence once more. As they turned to enter their house Kodua suddenly had an idea. His face brightened and he hit his chest with his hand. 'I'm going to build an ark,' he announced to his surprised friend.

'An a...a...ark?'

'Yes, like Noah's Ark. Only it's going to be my ark. Kodua's Ark,' Kodua said proudly.

'Are you all right?' Nyamesem asked in a worried voice.

'You think I'm mad, don't you? Well, I don't care. Everyone thought Noah was mad too.' Kodua paused and then without warning started to shout like a mad person. 'An ark, an ark, I'm going to build an ark!'

CHAPTER TWO

The next morning Kodua woke up feeling a bit silly. But the more he thought about building an ark, the more he liked the idea.

Kodua's Ark, bigger than all the other buildings in the village. He could see visitors from far and near coming to Mantu to see Kodua's Ark. Now he had the idea he knew exactly what he wanted to do. He had to plan how he was going to do it.

While he sat on the only stool in the house, thinking, Nyamesem got up, yawning. He fetched some water from the barrel and washed his face. Then he put some water in his mouth, rinsed it and spat it out between his teeth. He sat on the bare floor beside Kodua.

'Now, Mr Noah, I hope a good night's sleep has helped you. You realise that the idea of building an ark is extremely stupid, don't you?' he said with a grin. 'If it were so simple, everyone would build an ark and become famous.'

Kodua breathed in the morning air and smiled.

'I'm going to build an ark,' he insisted.

'But don't you see? It's impossible!'

'Nothing is impossible.'

'All right, Mr Noah, tell me how you're going to

do it,' Nyamesem challenged.

'I don't know – yet,' Kodua said truthfully.

'There! Look, just forget this madness.' Nyamesem stopped and seemed to get an idea, for his face brightened up.

'Why don't we go to Mame Ataa's bar? TK owes me a hundred cedis. We could buy a bottle of palm wine to drown our sorrows.'

'I don't drink palm wine,' Kodua said without smiling. That only made Nyamesem laugh.

'Since when?'

'Since yesterday when I decided to build an ark.'

'Who says you have to stop drinking palm wine to be able to build an ark?' Nyamesem asked.

'No one is going to make a fool of me any more. From now on, no more booze. I'm going to do something with my life. I'm going to be rich and famous. And I'm starting now.'

Nyamesem roared with laughter. Then he started to clap. 'Bravo, bravo,' he began. 'Now you tell me this. What are you going to build the ark with?'

Kodua thought for a while.

'Bamboo!' he said suddenly.

As soon as he said it he knew he was right. Bamboo was strong and there was lots of it in Mantu. In fact, there was a bamboo forest behind the primary school. Kodua had another idea.

'I know exactly where we can build the ark. On the no-man's land behind the primary school. It's close to the bamboo forest. It'll be perfect.'

For the first time, Nyamesem showed some interest in the plan. He nodded and said, 'A bamboo ark. That sounds good.'

'Welcome to Kodua's Ark,' Kodua laughed.

'Wait a minute,' Nyamesem said. He had stopped smiling. 'Aren't we forgetting something?'

'What?'

'Money. Where are we going to get money to hire all the carpenters and the other workers?' Nyamesem asked.

'Don't worry. We can do it,' Kodua replied. 'Come on, let's go and earn some money so that we can start.'

They both knew that there was only one way in which they could earn any money at all. Farmers hired labourers on a daily scale. It was called a 'by-day' job. Almost all the young men in Mantu took these jobs during the farming season. The two walked to the market place where all those who hoped to be employed for the day waited for the farmers. A group of five boys was waiting at the far end.

As soon as the boys saw Kodua and Nyamesem they started to shout.

Kodua ignored them. He really wanted to get a job. If he could build the ark, he wouldn't care about all those who teased him.

'Hey, KK, what do you want here? There's no palm wine here!' shouted a tall young man called Afuom Danso.

Kodua just smiled and shouted back, 'I didn't come for palm wine. I came for work just like you.'

Danso approached the two friends. He took Kodua's shirt collar and shook him hard.

'We don't need you here, so just disappear. There isn't enough work to go round,' he shouted.

Kodua remained calm. He had no other choice. He had to make some money. Besides, Danso was too big and strong for him. So he said nothing and waited until Danso released him.

'I'm warning you, KK, if you don't leave now, you'll regret it. I really mean it,' Danso said.

'I'm sorry. I can't leave. I need the work just as much as you do,' Kodua replied.

The other boys had now gathered around. Two of them started to heckle Kodua.

'Leave him alone!' Nyamesem said.

'Nobody will hire him anyway,' said Danso suddenly. 'I'll make sure of that.'

'I just want a chance,' said Kodua. 'I didn't come here to fight.'

Just as Kodua had said that, he saw a woman approaching them. She carried a basket and a machete and it was obvious she was looking for a labourer. She stopped near the group.

'I need two strong boys to handle my farm,' she said.

'We'll do it, madam,' Kodua said promptly.

'You, KK? Don't make me laugh,' said the woman. 'Do you even know how to hold a machete?'

'We'll charge you half the going rate, my friend and I,' said Kodua suddenly. The woman became interested.

'Are you sure?' she asked.

'He can't do that,' snapped Danso.

'Why not? It's a free country,' said the woman. She turned to Kodua. 'You two are hired. Let's go.'

But before Kodua could move, Danso seized him once again. Then, without warning, he hit Kodua on the mouth.

'Ouch!' Kodua screamed. He spat out blood and realised that one of his teeth had been knocked out.

'That'll teach you some sense,' Danso said and started to move away.

Kodua bent down holding his mouth in pain.

'You see what you've done,' Nyamesem complained. Danso laughed.

Then, without warning, he hit Kodua on the mouth.

'So what are you going to do about it?' he asked, pushing Nyamesem hard. His four friends cheered him on.

Meanwhile the woman, Yaayaa, was annoyed and spoke angrily to Danso and his friends.

'You didn't need to do that,' she said. 'I'm not going to hire any of you for this.'

'Keep your stupid job,' said Danso. 'I can go to the city any time and get an office job.'

'You do that. Because I'm keeping this farm job for Kodua and Nyamesem. And there's a lot to do.'

She turned to Kodua.

'Go on home and rest,' she said. 'Tomorrow I'll fetch the two of you and you can start working on the farm.'

She lowered her basket, took a piece of yam from it and gave it to Kodua. Then she turned away before Kodua could react.

'Thank you,' he said as the woman walked off.

The two friends returned home happier than before. Neither Kodua nor Nyomesem had eaten yam for over six months. They just couldn't afford it. It was almost like Christmas!

◇

They woke up at dawn the next day and waited for Yaayaa to fetch them. Kodua was excited. His mouth still hurt a bit but he found that all the other aches and pains he usually had were gone. By the time they got to the farm, the sun was rising. But the air was cool and the birds were still singing. It would be some time before it got hot.

'Now let's agree on the work,' Yaayaa said, after she had examined the farm. 'It will take you at least ten days to do the job. So if I pay you two hundred cedis each per day, that's four thousand cedis. I'll give you half after you finish today.'

'B-but ...' Kodua began. He was amazed. The work looked easy enough. The weeds that had started to grow were still quite short. Kodua guessed it would take them no more than seven or eight days to complete the work.

When he was finally able to speak, Kodua thanked Yaayaa. The woman was a middle-aged widow who'd never had children. Many people in Mantu avoided her because they thought she was a witch. But she was quite well off and had several farms, two of which she had inherited from her late husband.

It took Kodua and Nyamesem exactly eight days to finish the work. And they were richer by four thousand cedis. Neither of them had seen or held so much money in all their lives. Now, work on Kodua's Ark could begin. But there was a problem.

'Why should it be called Kodua's Ark?' Nyamesem asked. 'Half of the money is mine.'

'Here's your share,' Kodua said promptly.

'I don't want my share. I want us to work together.'

'In that case we work together. But the ark remains Kodua's Ark.'

'Oh, all right,' replied Nyamesem.

Kodua wanted to start at once. With Yaayaa's money and other work they had done since, they had nearly five thousand cedis! In the city it was just an average monthly wage, but it was a lot of money in Mantu. And they had Yaayaa to thank for that.

In the evening, Kodua had an idea. But his friend was worried.

'You want the village announcer to announce to the whole village that you want to build an ark?' Nyamesem asked.

'Sure. What's wrong with that? Come on, let's go and see Agya Manu.'

The two of them approached the house of Agya Manu, the village announcer, nervously. The old man was known to have a bad temper. It was shortly past sunset but they could see one lantern in the courtyard. Agya Manu sat on a stool by the lantern.

'What do you want in my house, KK?' he said

before they had a chance to greet him.

'Good evening,' Kodua said politely.

'I said what do you want here? I don't need any bad luck in my house. You've never been here before so why now?' said the old man. He took the pipe from his mouth and rubbed his bald head. He called to his dog.

'Please, we come in peace. I want you to beat the gong-gong and announce something for me,' said Kodua.

'You? KK boozeman? Get out of my house, both of you, before I set my dog on you,' Agya Manu snapped and started patting the dog. He pointed to Kodua and Nyamesem and the dog began to bark loudly.

Kodua didn't know whether to start running. Then he had an idea. He took out some money from his pocket.

'I'll reward you well, of course,' he said.

As soon as the old man saw the money, he pushed the dog away.

'Come and sit down here, young men. I may be able to help you after all.' He waited for the two to sit down. 'Now what can I do for you?'

'I want you to announce to the people of Mantu that I, Kojo Kodua, am going to build an ark,' Kodua said.

'An ark? B-but ...'

Kodua pushed five hundred cedis into the old man's palm. That was five times the normal charge.

'Of course, whatever you say. If you want me to say you're Noah come back to life, I'll say it. That's my job.'

'Just say I am going to build an ark, right here in Mantu,' Kodua said. 'We'll come back in about an hour. We want to be with you when you're doing it.'

'Anything you say,' said Agya Manu. 'Anything you say.'

Later that evening the two went to see Agya Manu again. The old man was now extremely nice.

'Hello, my nephews, come in,' he said. He was dressed up as he always was when he was going to beat the gong-gong. He wore a white T-shirt over a pair of large black shorts. And he had his gong-gong and stick in hand. He handed the gong-gong and stick to Kodua to carry.

It was the custom that the announcer must start all announcements near the palace. The chief of Mantu, Nana Badu, was out of the village. But that didn't change the custom.

Agya Manu struck his gong-gong several times when they got near the palace. He waited for a while and struck it again. Soon a small group of people gathered around. Then he began the announcement.

'Good people of Mantu, take note,' he started, as he always did. 'You all know our beloved friend and nephew Kojo Kodua ...'

Chants of 'KK boozeman!' started from the small crowd. When the chants died down, Agya Manu continued.

'Our nephew Kodua is about to do something that no son or daughter of Mantu has ever done or dreamt of doing ...' he paused. Now there was silence. 'He is about to do what only one man has ever done. He's going to build an ark ...'

'An ark!' several people shouted. Then there was a roar of laughter. The idea seemed to shock and amuse the people at the same time. Soon the crowd broke up into small groups. They stood arguing among themselves. Kodua was not sure what they were saying, but he heard the word 'mad' several times.

The crowd that followed them got bigger and bigger as they moved from one spot to another announcing the news. Soon they came to a part of the village where most of the richer people lived.

'Good people of Mantu ...' Agya Manu began.

'Shut up, old man!' someone shouted. Out of the darkness came a young man carrying a powerful

'He's going to build an ark ...'

torchlight. It was Afuom Danso.

'Enough of this nonsense, old man.' Danso turned to Kodua. 'As for you, boozeman, you will not build any ark in this village as long as I'm here.' He shone the torch into Kodua's eyes and pushed him aside. Then he walked away.

The old man continued his announcement as soon as Danso left. Now the sky was very dark and the few stars that had been visible earlier had disappeared.

Kodua knew that the hard work was just starting. Even so, he was happy. For the first time in years some people actually shook his hand and congratulated him on his idea. He felt happy. The crowd broke up when Agya Manu finished the announcement. The old man's voice was now almost hoarse with shouting. Kodua shook his hand and thanked him.

As he turned, someone poured liquid on his head and in his eyes. Some of it went into his mouth. It was urine and it smelled terrible! He saw someone run into the darkness but he couldn't tell who it was.

CHAPTER THREE

On the Friday morning Kodua and Nyamesem got up early to visit the empty space behind the primary school. Part of the plot was grassland but a large part was covered in bushes. As he stood there, Kodua realised that there was a lot of very hard work ahead. First, a large area had to be cleared. Then the bamboo trees had to be cut and carried to the site.

'We can't clear this place all by ourselves. We need to get some help,' said Kodua.

They decided to spend the rest of the day clearing as much of the plot as possible. Then they could find help the next day. But before they began work, the two friends went to see one of the village carpenters, who lived near the primary school.

They explained what they wanted.

'As a matter of fact, I made a signboard for someone two weeks ago but he hasn't come to collect it. I could give you that and make another one for him,' Mr Safo said. He brought a large board fixed to a pole.

Kodua nodded as he inspected it.

'Yes, this will be perfect,' he said. He turned to Nyamesem. 'What do you think?'

'I suppose,' said Nyamesem.

'Can't you sound a little happier than that?'

'Well, why should I? It's all yours, isn't it? Kodua's Ark. What has it got to do with me?' Nyamesem said.

Kodua placed his hand on Nyamesem's shoulder and asked him what the matter was. Was he still upset that the ark would be named after Kodua? But Nyamesem remained silent. Suddenly he pushed Kodua's hand away and walked off. Kodua went after him, but Nyamesem would not speak to him. Kodua returned to Mr Safo's shop.

'Can you write on the signboard?' he asked.

'Of course. What do you want me to write?'

' "Site for Kodua's Ark. Please keep off ".'

'It'll soon be ready. Now let's talk about money.'

◇

Kodua went back to the site and started to clear away the bushes. Nyamesem's behaviour worried him and made him want to give up, especially when he considered how much more work there was to do. But he also knew that, having made the announcement, there was no turning back.

Soon after he started work the sun began to shine brightly. He felt hot but continued to work. He had worked hard the past ten days. But when he thought how famous he would be, he felt strong. After all, he had managed to put on some weight since he resolved to do something with his life.

When Safo brought the signboard, he told Kodua how silly his ideas were.

'Don't make a fool of yourself,' he advised.

'It can't get worse,' said Kodua, with a smile. 'I'm already a fool in Mantu.'

'Don't say I didn't warn you,' Safo said. He took his money and went away.

During the ten o'clock break, several of the children from the primary school and the junior secondary school came to watch him. Soon there was a large crowd of excited school children all around. Some of them shouted. But several stood silently just watching. Finally one boy, about twelve years old, approached Kodua.

'Please, can I help you?' he asked.

Kodua thought for a moment.

'Sure! What's your name?' he asked.

'Boafo,' he said.

'All right, Boafo. Do you see that signboard over there?' He pointed to the board. 'Plant it in the ground for me.'

'All right,' the boy said excitedly. He ran to the board and looked around for a machete. The boys around him produced three machetes. Several other boys stepped forward to help and within a few minutes the signboard had been planted firmly.

Within a few minutes the signboard had been planted firmly.

Before noon Nyamesem came back.

'I'm sorry I behaved that way,' he apologised.

'I'm glad you're back. There's a lot of work to be done,' said Kodua, shaking his friend's hand.

◇

In the afternoon, several of the boys brought machetes and set about clearing the weeds. It was hard work but the children were fighting to take part. Kodua was pleased. He knew now that Kodua's Ark was not only his dream. It seemed to be the children's dream too. He owed it to himself and these children to make the dream come true.

By the end of the day almost all the grassland portion of the site had been cleared. Kodua was amazed at the amount of work they had been able to do, and he was extremely grateful to the children.

Boafo came up to him and asked if he could go and cut some bamboo.

'How do you know I'll use bamboo?' Kodua asked, surprised.

'If I were going to build an ark that would sit on land,' the boy said, 'I would use bamboo.'

'That's right.'

'Can I bring some bamboo tomorrow?' Boafo pleaded.

'All right, all right,' said Kodua.

The boy told another boy who told another boy. And soon the word had reached nearly everyone. Anyone who could, should bring one bamboo tree.

The next day was Saturday. Early in the morning Kodua and Nyamesem went to the site with a group of ten boys to clear the thicket. To his surprise all the boys declined to take any money for their work.

'It's our ark too,' they said. 'Just give us lunch.'

Kodua bought the boys some boiled yams and rice from the market.

With so much enthusiasm, the work took very little time. Soon the whole site was completely cleared. Then as they sat down to rest, the children started bringing in the bamboo. First they came one at a time. Then they came in a long line. It was as if all the children in Mantu were helping.

'We must give the kids something to eat. That's the least they deserve,' Kodua told Nyamesem.

'I'll go and get mashed *kenkey* with sugar,' said Nyamesem, getting up.

'Go to Yaayaa and buy some *kenkey* and get someone to mash it properly,' said Kodua. Then he saw Yaayaa coming towards them. She carried something on her head.

As it turned out, Yaayaa had already done the job. She brought a large bowl full of mashed *kenkey* with sugar.

'It's for the children,' she said. And she wouldn't take any money.

The food helped the children to work harder. Very soon most of the site was covered with bamboo. The real work of building the ark could now begin.

◇

When he received a summons to see the chief on Monday, Kodua was very pleased. The chief had been out of the village for the past month.

'I feel very proud that the chief has called me to the palace,' Kodua said. He put on the new shirt he had bought the week before and set off with Nyamesem to see the chief. It was one of his proudest moments.

As they walked along the side street towards the chief's palace they met a group of boys led by Afuom Danso. The boys stopped right in front of Kodua and Nyamesem, blocking their path.

'I warned you, KK,' Danso said.

'You can't touch me,' said Kodua, 'or I'll report you to the chief and you'll be in serious trouble.'

'What does the chief care about you, boozeman?'

'If you must know, the chief is very interested in my plans,' said Kodua.

'Stupid fool, who gave you that idea?' Danso asked, laughing.

'Why else would he invite me to his palace?'

Danso seemed shocked at the news. For a moment he looked rather confused. Then he grinned.

'I'm not through with you yet. And next time it may not be just urine in your face.'

'Excuse me,' said Kodua, and he walked away.

The officials refused to allow Nyamesem to accompany Kodua into the palace. They said that the chief wanted to see Kodua and not his friend.

It was a large house with a wide courtyard. There were several leather chairs neatly arranged along a veranda. Kodua was ushered through a door into a large hall.

'Sit down here,' said one of the officials. 'Nana will be with you shortly.'

It was several minutes before the chief entered the hall, with five other men. The two men who were in the room with Kodua stood up and Kodua followed. The chief sat down and waved everyone else to do the same.

Kodua stood up again.

'I want to thank the chief for–'

'Be quiet!' one official shouted. 'Who said you could speak?'

Kodua was surprised.

'I was just– '

'I said be quiet!'

He sat down, still not quite sure what all the fuss was about. The chief waved to the official and said he would speak directly to Kodua. Kodua watched the man in admiration. He was about forty and extremely handsome.

'I understand you are building an ark,' the chief said suddenly.

'Yes, sir, Nana. It's going to be a wonderful– '

'Just answer my questions,' the chief snapped.

A fly buzzed around his ears and Kodua flapped it away. He could not understand the chief's change of attitude.

'Who gave you that piece of land you're planning to use?'

'I ... I ... Nobody gave it to me. I thought the place was a kind of no-man's land,' Kodua said. He waved away the troublesome fly once more.

'What a fool you are, Kodua. All land belongs to somebody. No-man's land belongs to the chief of Mantu who keeps it safe for the people,' said the chief. 'If you want to use it you must pay.'

Kodua realised that there was no point beating about the bush. The chief was not on his side as he had thought. And he had not invited him to the palace to congratulate him.

'How much?' Kodua asked.

'Be quiet!' shouted the official again.

'But why– ?' Kodua stopped in mid sentence as the fly flew straight into his mouth. He quickly spat it out and was horrified when saliva from his mouth flew straight into the chief's face.

Two officials seized him instantly and forced him into a kneeling position.

'Nana, your humble servant, Kodua, begs for forgiveness. He's sorry for what he has done and promises to slaughter a sheep to pay for his rudeness,' said the short official who had been shouting at Kodua.

Slaughter a sheep, Kodua thought as the two men let him go.

'I'm sorry, Chief,' Kodua said, trying to stand up.

'Be more careful. Now about the land, you will have to pay the sum of one hundred thousand cedis.'

Kodua nearly fainted. One hundred thousand cedis! He would have to save *all* his daily wages for a full year and more before he could ever hope to save so much. He decided to appeal to the chief's kindness. After all, when the ark was built it would attract visitors to Mantu and all the people would benefit.

He got up from his chair and approached the chief's stool until he was standing right in front of the noble man. He bent low in respect and raised himself again. Kodua had moved before any of the officials could stop him.

'I have an appeal to make ...' he began, moving

closer to the chief.

Four of the officials jumped forward and held Kodua. This time they forced him to lie flat on his face while they kicked him from all sides.

◇

He was detained in a small windowless room in the palace with no lantern. It was the most terrible night he had ever spent.

In the morning two of the officials came to see him. When they opened the door the light flooded the room and Kodua had to shut his eyes for some time. He came out of the room feeling very sore.

'Look at his face, it's like a monkey's,' said the short official.

'Stupid fool. How dare you go near the chief of Mantu?' the other echoed. 'You're lucky the chief is a generous man. Be thankful he has given you the lightest of punishments.'

'Punishment? After all this?' Kodua said tearfully.

'You're very lucky. It's been decided that you must slaughter five sheep. That'll cost you ten thousand cedis. And if you still want to build your stupid ark you can have the land for half the price, only fifty thousand cedis. You have only three days to provide the ten thousand cedis. If you don't, you will be banished from Mantu – for ever.'

CHAPTER FOUR

When Kodua got home he threw himself on his mat and went to sleep. It was only when he got up several hours later that he saw Nyamesem sitting on the mat beside him.

'Where were you? I was so worried about you, but they refused to let me into the palace,' said Nyamesem. 'What happened?'

Kodua gave a deep sigh and told his friend the story.

'They slapped and kicked and punched me. And they still want me to pay ten thousand cedis within three days. We only have about three thousand cedis left. Where can I get seven thousand before Thursday? And I'm too weak even to work.'

'There're only three people in Mantu who could find that kind of money in such a short time. Manager Bempah, Mame Ataa and Yaayaa,' said Nyamesem.

'The first two are out. Which leaves Yaayaa.'

'Unfortunately she's out of the village. I saw her leaving in a truck yesterday. She's gone to Salaga market and may be away for nearly a week,' said Nyamesem.

Kodua was suddenly afraid. He knew he could

not go to Manager Bempah. Mame Ataa, though not exactly an angel, was his last hope. Maybe she could lend him seven thousand cedis to pay to the chief. As for the fifty thousand cedis for the plot of land, it could wait. The ark would have to wait. Maybe a year or two. Now he had to make sure that he was not banished from Mantu. For he knew he had nowhere else to go.

After lunch Kodua and Nyamesem went to Mame Ataa's bar. There was silence as they entered. Then someone shouted, 'Long time no see, KK!'

Kodua just smiled and greeted the merry drinkers.

Then he smelt the alcohol. He had stopped drinking when he decided to build the ark, but he would have taken a drink now. He shook his head. He was determined not to go back to drinking.

He greeted Mame Ataa and whispered into her ear.

'Come to the inner room,' she invited. 'Alone.'

Kodua went behind the counter and entered the inner room Mame Ataa kept as a kind of office. He decided not to beat about the bush. So he told her about his ordeal and asked for a loan of seven thousand cedis.

'You want seven thousand cedis?' she asked.

'Yes, Mame Ataa. I promise to pay within a short

time,' Kodua said. He held his breath as he waited for the answer.

She thought for a while and said, 'Certainly. Wait here.' Then she went out of the room back to the counter to serve the customers.

Kodua waited for over half an hour before Mame Ataa returned to the room. She sat in the large chair opposite Kodua, wiping sweat from her face every now and then.

'Have you eaten today?' Mame Ataa asked suddenly.

'Yes, I have.' Kodua was pleasantly surprised by the question.

'Did you sleep well yesterday?'

He shook his head and said, 'Not a wink. I had a most terrible night, as I've said.'

'I thought as much,' said Mame Ataa. She opened her bag and took out a wad of notes, which she began to count. When she finished she handed the money over to Kodua to count.

'Exactly seven thousand cedis,' he said excitedly. 'Thank you very much, Mame Ataa. You'll never regret this.'

She stretched her hand and took the money back. 'You're sure you have eaten today?'

'Yes, thank you,' said Kodua.

'Then it must be the lack of sleep that is driving

you crazy,' said Mame Ataa. She put the money back in her bag. Kodua was now confused.

'Please, Mame Ataa, I ... I don't understand ...'

'Do you understand this?' She brought out an old piece of paper. Kodua recognised the five poorly drawn lines and remembered that he still owed the woman five hundred cedis. He had just forgotten. He had not been back since giving up palm wine.

He tried to smile and said, 'I'm sorry. I forgot.'

He took five hundred cedis from his pocket. She took it and put it in her bag.

'Now get out!' she shouted.

'Oh, Mame Ataa, please!'

'Did you think I would lend money to you? I know you well. You're no good. So whether you build a ship or a bomb, you can't deceive me. Now get out.'

Kodua got up and left the room without another word.

◇

They saw several other people, but were only able to borrow a total of three thousand cedis. The rumour was all over the town that Kodua was going to be banished from Mantu. Many of the people avoided him. There was only one thing to do. He would present the total of six thousand cedis that he had to the officials and ask them to accept it.

Or ask them to give him more time to pay. He could do nothing more.

He went to bed late for he and Nyamesem had sat talking into the night.

It was nearly dawn when Kodua finally fell asleep. But his sleep was soon disturbed by bangs on the door. When he opened it, six officials from the palace were waiting for him.

'We've been asked to bring you to the palace now,' said the short one. Immediately they seized him and started dragging him away. Nyamesem heard the noise and got up. He ran after them, but he was pushed violently aside.

As they took him away a few people gathered and followed them from a distance.

But when they got to the chief's palace, everything had changed. The chief came to meet him and shake hands with him. He waved the officials away and offered Kodua a seat.

'I'm sorry about what happened to you yesterday,' the chief said. 'These people are worried someone will attack me. Also the elders of the court wouldn't allow me to give the land away for nothing. But it's all right now that someone has paid for it for you.'

'Someone has paid for everything?' Kodua gasped.

'Everything. The fine and the land. But the person has asked to remain anonymous. So don't ask me who it was.'

Kodua nodded. He had a good idea who it was. But how Yaayaa had managed to do it he could not understand, for she was still away from Mantu.

◇

The building of the ark started again the next day. All the volunteers flocked back to the site. It was a wonderful sight. Almost the whole village came at one time or another.

The two village carpenters and their apprentices came and worked free of charge. The farmers brought yams and plantains. Some women cooked them at the site and everybody had enough to eat. Kodua had the hardest job organising the work.

Two more weeks passed. The floor of the ark was completed. Ninety metres long and fifty metres wide. Several pieces of hardwood were now needed for pillars and as a frame on which to build the bamboo skin.

Kodua's secret friend came to their rescue once more. Money was provided through the chief to buy wood.

The way the ark took shape amazed Kodua. In the beginning he had only a vague idea how the

The way the ark took shape amazed Kodua.

thing should look. But as they worked the ark looked just right.

Everyone agreed that this particular ark was not going to be a zoo for animals since they didn't expect a flood. But it would be a kind of museum or exhibition centre for antiques, works of art and other precious things.

After another few weeks the ark was growing. It was now several metres tall and a few of the rooms had already been built. One day Yaayaa came to see what was happening.

'But why did you decide to build an *ark*?' she asked. 'It's most unusual, isn't it? An ark?'

'It just came into my head.'

'Rubbish!' someone shouted from behind. It was Afuom Danso. He was wearing a beret and a T-shirt with a badly written inscription – No Stupid Ark!

'Don't mind Danso. He's just jealous,' Kodua told Yaayaa.

'Jealous of what? All you have done is to get some poor school children to waste their time on this stupid project,' Danso said. 'Someone's got to stop you.' He turned and ran off towards the village.

◇

Kodua was wakened in the night by bangs on the door. When he opened it there were several people in the courtyard. They were all shouting excitedly and Kodua could not hear a word.

'The ark, the ark ... is on fire!' someone shouted.

Kodua stared for a moment. Then he shouted, 'What's happened?'

'The ark is on fire. Someone set it alight ...'

Kodua stood still for an instant, then without another word he ran through the darkness. He didn't stop until he came to the building site. The night sky was lit by the fire that was burning brightly. There was smoke everywhere.

He stood watching the ark go up in flames. His dream, his hopes. The dream of the people of Mantu. He pushed his way through the crowd of people who had gathered there.

'Do something, you people, do something!' he screamed. Then he saw several people with buckets of water standing helplessly by. He grabbed a bucket and ran to the place where the fire was highest. But it was so hot that he couldn't get near enough to throw the water into the fire.

'It's no use,' said a woman standing close by. 'It's no use.'

Her voice was filled with sadness. The ark was her dream too. And now it was on fire.

Nyamesem got to the site several minutes later and stood by Kodua, panting. He was also

He broke the chain and went sadly home.

speechless as he watched the blaze.

'Let's go back home,' Nyamesem suggested. 'We can't do anything about the fire.'

'Go on home if you like. I can't leave my ark.'

Together with a small group of people, Kodua stayed around until the morning. More people joined them until almost the whole village was there. The school children came in their uniforms and stood to watch the ruins on their way to school. The fire had burnt itself out, but little of the structure remained. A piece of bamboo here, a piece of hardwood there. That was all.

Some of the children started to hold hands. And soon a chain began to form. They stretched out until a human chain had formed completely with the ruins in the middle. But it was now too much for Kodua. He broke the chain and went sadly home.

He refused to eat anything for three days. He would go and sit at the site from the morning till late at night before coming home. Then he began to spend the night on the ground in the cold. He grew weaker and weaker and started to cough.

Exactly one week after the ark was burnt Kodua was taken to the hospital in the city, seriously ill.

CHAPTER FIVE

After a few days in the hospital, Kodua began to feel better. The cough and chest pains stopped, and he wasn't so feverish.

In the end he spent ten days there. The doctor told him when he was going to go home. Kodua told Nyamesem, who was the only person who had visited him regularly.

The day before he went home, he started to worry about his bill. But Nyamesem told him not to worry as the bill was going to be paid by a friend. But Nyamesem would not tell Kodua the name of this person.

Kodua left the hospital one Wednesday afternoon. In a way he was sorry to be going back home. The hospital had made him forget his sorrow at the burning of the ark. Now that he was going back to Mantu all the pain returned.

'I wish I could go somewhere else,' Kodua said as he and Nyamesem walked down the stairs. 'I wish I could remain in the city and find work.'

'Life in the city can be rough for those without a good job, or any job at all,' Nyamesem said

'How would you know?'

'My uncle used to live here once. He came back

to Mantu to farm,' Nyamesem replied. 'He lived with a friend for a year, sleeping in a bare corridor because his friend had only one room and a large family.'

They walked a mile or so from the hospital to the big lorry park. The park was one huge muddy mess thanks to the rains of the past few days. The two friends walked slowly towards Mantu station.

The wooden truck was nearly full but Kodua and Nyamesem were able to find seats. The back of the truck was loaded with food and other goods. A strong smell of fish filled the air.

'KK boozeman!' someone shouted suddenly.

Kodua's heart gave a jump. For ten whole days he had had some peace. Now he was having to go back to Mantu to face the shouts and laughter all over again. When the building of the ark was going smoothly, almost everybody became his friend. But now that the ark was burnt, it was going to be tough for him in Mantu again.

He turned to Nyamesem and whispered, 'Let's stay in the city. We'll be much better off.'

But Nyamesem wouldn't hear of it.

'We must go back to Mantu. That's where our future is.'

'Future!' Kodua shouted. 'What future? The ark was our future. Look what happened to it!'

'You were the one who taught me to have faith and hope. You insisted that we could make it if we believed in ourselves. And now you want to quit?' Nyamesem asked.

The lorry started with a jerk. The engine revved and the two-hour journey to Mantu began.

'You can't quit now,' Nyamesem added.

'Quit what? I just want a fresh start. Is that quitting?' Kodua replied angrily. 'At least I made a try of it. And while it lasted, I showed the people of Mantu that KK is not a useless animal!'

'Keep your voice down,' Nyamesem pleaded. He placed his arm on Kodua's shoulder. 'We can start to build the ark once more.'

'No! I have no money to start again. And how do you think we can get people to offer help once again? Everyone is tired of it. And it's all Afuom Danso's fault!' Kodua said angrily.

'You don't know for sure that he burnt down the ark.'

'Everyone knows but nobody is doing anything about it. You know, I feel like getting a gun and going over to his house to shoot him!' Kodua said.

'Don't talk like that!' Nyamesem scolded.

Kodua dozed on and off until they were at the outskirts of Mantu. When he saw some of the huts from the distance his heart started to beat fast. How he wished he could jump off the lorry and go back to the city. But now it was too late.

He said nothing until they got to the station. When the lorry stopped, Kodua jumped down quickly, intending to slip away quietly to avoid attracting attention. His heart nearly stopped when he saw Manager Bempah walking towards him, smiling.

What does he want now? Kodua wondered. He had never forgiven the man for making fun of him at Mame Ataa's bar.

'Hello, Kodua,' Bempah greeted.

'What now?' asked Kodua with a frown.

'Get into my car. I have something to tell you,' Bempah said. He reached out and put an arm around Kodua. But Kodua slowly pushed it away, still wondering what the man was up to. Just then Nyamesem got to the scene.

'Let's get into the car,' he urged Kodua.

Everything seemed strange. Kodua wanted to ask several questions but when he opened his mouth, no words came out. Seeing that Nyamesem was already walking towards Bempah's car he followed him and sat down in the back.

'What is this thing you wanted to talk to me about?' Kodua asked as the car started.

'First, I want you to know that I'm not your enemy,' Bempah said.

'Hah! If you're my friend, I don't want to meet my enemies!' Kodua retorted.

'He paid the ten thousand cedis to the chief for you,' Nyamesem said.

'He didn't,' Kodua said in disbelief.

'He also paid the full cost of the land on which the ark was to have been built. Fifty thousand cedis.'

Kodua opened his mouth.

'Er ... er ... thank you,' was all he could say.

'I enjoyed it. Anyway, how would you like to build a new, bigger ark?' Bempah asked.

'Ha ... how?'

They turned on to a small side road that led to the primary school. There seemed to be hundreds of school children waiting.

'What's going on?' Kodua asked.

'They're waiting for you,' Bempah said.

'Me? They're waiting for me?'

The car came to a stop. Bempah got out quickly and opened the door for Kodua. As soon as Kodua left the car, several of the older school children mobbed him.

'KK! KK!' they shouted. They carried him on their

shoulders up to a low platform. Bempah and Nyamesem joined him up there. There were more cheers.

'Ladies and gentlemen, children, greetings!' Bempah began.

'We want KK! We want KK!' they shouted.

'You see, they love you,' Nyamesem said.

When there was silence, Bempah continued.

'We've gathered today to welcome back our hero KK ...'

'KK! KK!' the crowd shouted.

'He's an inspiration to all the young people of Mantu. That's why we have decided that he needs our support. So I, Manager Bempah, have decided to give the money to build a new ark. We will use good quality wood throughout. And it will be called Kodua's Ark.'

Kodua could not believe his ears. He couldn't keep the tears out of his eyes.

'And now, Kodua will make a speech,' Bempah said.

Speech? He wondered what he could say. Kodua surveyed the crowd. He caught sight of Afuom Danso near the front, waving excitedly. Then he started to smile ...

'We want KK! We want KK!' they shouted.

Questions

1 What is Kodua famous for in the village?

2 What makes Kodua decide to do something different, like building an ark?

3 Who are the people who help Kodua? How do they help him?

4 Why do Mame Ataa and Danso treat Kodua so badly?

5 Why do the court officials throw Kodua into the little room for the night?

6 Kodua and Nyamesem fall out twice. What do they fight about?

7 Why does Kodua want to build an ark? Why not an ordinary boat or a house or something like that?

8 The villagers and the children always used to make fun of Kodua. So why do they now help him to build the ark?

Activities

1 Draw a picture of an ark, either when it is finished or as it is being built. Try to find pictures of Noah's Ark.

2 Write a short story about a rescue by boat. You are the person who is rescued.

Glossary

abdomen (page 2) your stomach, your tummy

announcer (page 25) the person who tells the people in the village all the news

banished (page 41) sent away from a place and told never to come back again

boozeman (page 1) someone who drinks a lot of alcohol

going rate (page 21) the amount of money normally paid for doing a job

jerk (page 55) a sudden sharp movement

kenkey (page 36) popular Ghanaian food made from boiled corn dough

machete (page 21) a large knife with a heavy blade for cutting

summons (page 37) an instruction to appear before a judge or a chief

The Junior African Writers Series is designed to provide interesting and varied African stories both for pleasure and for study. There are five graded levels in the series.

Level 3 is for readers who have been studying English for five to six years. The content and language have been carefully controlled to increase fluency in reading.

Content The plots are linear in development and only the characters and information central to the storyline are introduced. Chapters divide the stories into focused episodes and the illustrations help the reader to picture the scenes.

Language Reading is a learning experience and, although the choice of words is carefully controlled, new words, important to the story, are also introduced. These are contextualised, recycled through the story and explained in the glossary. The sentences contain a maximum of three clauses.

Glossary Difficult words which learners may not know and which are not made clear in the text or illustrations have been listed alphabetically at the back of the book. The definitions refer to the way the word is used in the story and the page reference is for the word's first use.

Questions and **Activities** The questions give useful comprehension practice and ensure that the reader has followed and understood the story. The activities develop themes and ideas introduced and can be done as pairwork or groupwork in class, or as homework.